THE BAMBOO PRINCESS
AND THE
MUSIC HANDS MAN

Based on The Bamboo Cutter's Tale

by

DoAnn T. Kaneko

Edited by Dona Snow
Illustrated by Lance Williams

AuthorHouse™
1663 Liberty Drive, Suite 200
Bloomington, IN 47403
www.authorhouse.com
Phone: 1-800-839-8640

First published by AuthorHouse 9/3/2008
ISBN: 978-1-4343-6511-8 (sc)

Printed in the United States of America
Bloomington, Indiana

This book is printed on acid-free paper.

author**HOUSE**®

AUTHOR'S FOREWORD

The story of The Bamboo Princess and The Music Hands Man is based on the Japanese Fairy story called "Taketori Monogatari - The Bamboo Cutter's Tale" written in the Heian period (794-1192). I was very young when my mother first read me the story of a tiny baby girl emerging from a stalk of bamboo. Of course, I was amazed and fascinated by such a startling description. I knew that babies did not grow out of bamboo, but my imagination was captured, and I was carried away by the story my mother read to me. As an adult, I realize that all of us – but especially young children - can be captivated by the wonder and surprise of fairy tales, and the imaginative tales of fantasy and science fiction. Such stories almost put us into a trance state where we can automatically accept the wondrous fantasies such as a baby girl emerging from bamboo, or a talking pumpkin, a flying horse, or an ET falling to earth from a spaceship.

Pleasure and delight is a cross-cultural, universal response to stories of fantasy and magical fiction. These stories simultaneously instruct and delight; for while our imagination soars with the fantastic story, we are receiving lessons about real life. In ET and Princess Bamboo we are drawn right in by captivating storytelling as each story offers profound and important lessons about real life. Both ET and Princess Bamboo are so innocent, and kindhearted that they inspire love and attachment from all who meet them, but the attachment they inspire in others cannot hold them here on earth. Like all of us, ET and Princess Bamboo, are here on earth only temporarily. The love they inspire and experience may endure and grow over time, but neither force nor attachment can hold them here forever. The Princess returns to the moon, and ET returns to his home. This is a truth and a destiny we all share: each one of us must return to the universe. The important lessons embedded in both ET and

Princess Bamboo demonstrate that love and courage and compassion are the real treasures that endure and create meaning in our lives.

The story of a rabbit making rice cakes on the moon is another fairy tale from my youth. As children, we would look up at the moon, and on the surface of the moon we would find the shape of the rabbit with long ears. Across the world, people look up at the night sky with awe and wonder. Moonlight replaces the ordinary, sometimes harsh, light of the day with a gentle and silvery alternate light offered to us at night time. Moonlight, softly gently glowing, offers our imagination a multitude of possibilities, an almost infinite array of 'magical' and visionary possibility that can expand our reality. From my own childhood too, I have another strong memory. In the everyday light of the real world of my classroom, I always saw a beautiful little girl. She was as real as anyone else there, but to me she was so mysterious that she inspired my imagination to dream of moonlight and enchantment in my everyday, ordinary, school-time reality.

"Taketori Monogatari" touched my imagination so deeply that the story my mother read to me so long ago remains vivid to me today. This tale entertains both kids and adults alike as it demonstrates valuable lessons about caring, compassion, healing, teaching and helping others. The enchantment of moonlight encircles the story as the actions of Princess Bamboo and The Music Hands Man bring hope, healing, and peace into their community and their world.

As I began my journey in the healing arts, I developed a sense of reverence for the sun and the moon. In Chinese medicine, we define the sun as the master of Yang energy and the moon as master of Yin energy. The sun provides us with light and heat and causes the power of motion. The moon controls the ocean and composes the earth, causing peace. According to Taoism, we follow the divine order of the universe. According to Buddhism we follow the mystic law of the universe. All life depends on the power of the sun and the moon, the healing masters of the universe.

In my profession, I use artistic tapping techniques in Anma massage therapy in order to soothe the tension and pain that can be located in the shoulder, neck, and back. This tapping has great entertainment value as well as a therapeutic, healing power. My patients just love it. I recall how I used to practice the same techniques for my parents. It was my good fortune to be born in the second generation of these healing arts, so I could learn and develop very quickly without any obstacles. Also in my kindergarden, all of us in the class, used to sing a song along with this practice of tapping music hands, "Mom, let me tap your shoulder, Tan ton tan ton tan ton ton." It is called the Katatataki song. This tradition in our Asian countries is profound and spiritual. It is such a wonderful way to unite the family through body work and body language. This gives the family a great opportunity to help each other naturally. And, of course, it is wise to educate our children to practice love for elders and seniors in the family and in the community. This is the happiness of compassion and the wisdom of the mystic law of the universe: the law of the cause and effect. Good causes bring the effect of the good Karma of happiness.

I am pleased to be able to integrate my various backgrounds and disciplines through the vehicle of Taketori Monogatari and Katatataki songs. In the format of a simple but unforgettable story, I can offer examples of the healing art of magical music hands along with the practice of Buddhism; at the same time, this story demonstrates compassion in the family and healing in the community. It is a beautiful virtue to practice devotion to parents; this is called Oyakoko in Japanese. I adapted the original story by adding what I call 'monkey business.' This is the practice of the healing power of laughter. Fun and good health go together, increasing with laughter. And, the Katataki song reminds kids to practice on their parents and elders in the community.

The original story ended unhappily with the permanent disappointment of losing the Bamboo Princess. Instead, it was important to me to offer a positive, healing, peaceful message. In my ending, no one killed anyone, not even animals or insects. Non-violence is one of the most important principles of Buddhism. The nation whose people know about healing hands, and compassion and wisdom, will prevail in peace and happiness. This is very possible through the family practice of music, magic hands, and Buddhism.

ACKNOWLEDGMENT

My inspiration for exploring the universe through Taoism and Nichiren Buddhism is due to the great influences of many dear and gifted people who guided me to this level - including my parents Hideo and Kimie, my brother Sadao, my daughter Lisa, and friends and members from SGI. I would also like to express my deepest gratitude to two important people, the talented editor Dona Snow and illustrator Lance Williams. Indeed, my message has been realized in this beautiful picture book through my lovely student Dona who is studying Doin and Chigong in our Community class; she understands my mission in this field. I am fortunate to have her as an editor. She is a ceramic artist and English instructor with many connections to Japanese culture. She is committed to the ideals of healing and compassion as presented in this story. Lance's illustrations provide colorful images as I requested. He presents this fairy tale world with simple and appropriate images which I greatly enjoy. He also showed enthusiasm for the traditional healing arts and for community service.

I also express my gratitude to the AuthorHouse. Especially to Adalee Cooney for her heart felt professionalism. Their staff assisted me in reaching my goal successfully. I also would like to thank Lilly Craigen who helped with suggestions for my English in the early stages. I finally offer my appreciation to Susan Guralnik who is a graduate from our Shiatsu school. She assisted me in preparing everything for the Author's House, with such details as proofreading my corresponding materials and creating checkup lists. She really helped me a lot at the end of this overwhelming and demanding production process. Without the love and support of so many good people, I would never have been able to accomplish this dream.

DoAnn T.Kaneko Ph.D.,LAc.
September 2, 2008
www.chi-time.com

Once upon a time, somewhere faraway in the high mountains, there lived an old couple known locally as the Bamboo Crafts People. The old man, Mr. Bamboo-Cutter, gathered bamboo everyday in the forest. He was a very special artist. He could make sculptures of the Buddha out of bamboo. His wife took the sculptures to the market to sell.

The old couple was happy together, but they were also a little lonely, so they used to chant "Nam Myoho Renge Kyo" to the Gohonzon of Nichiren Buddhism every day. "Let us have a little girl to add to our family." But unfortunately, they were just too old now to have their own child.

One magical night under a full moon, Mr. Bamboo-Cutter was hurrying home to his wife after a long day of collecting bamboo. Although the bamboo was heavy and his back was aching, he always hurried home at a fast pace because he knew his wife was waiting for him to return. But, suddenly – on this one night – he was very startled as he came to the trail's end. The air was full of terrible, loud shouting sounds.

"Oh, my Goodness!" the old man whispered. "What on earth? What is going on here?"

He had never heard such a loud ruckus before. He peered through the leaves. There he saw a bunch of monkeys. They were jumping up and down, giggling, laughing, and pointing at something in the bamboo trees. Mr. Bamboo-Cutter could see a mysterious, golden light glowing in the bamboo trees.

"What on earth is that mysterious light … hummm,… and why are those silly monkeys so excited?" the old man wondered to himself.

"HAA-HAA!! HIHI-HU-HU HEEE-HOOOOOO!!"

The laughing sound of those monkeys was wild and weird. Mr. Bamboo-Cutter was just a little frightened, but he was also very curious.

"Well… well, those are very crazy monkeys! If they find me, who knows what they will do? I don't want to be teased with their wild laughing. I think I had better go right home. This is too strange, but tomorrow I will definitely return in the daylight."

The old Bamboo-Cutter rushed home and fell asleep immediately. He did not want to worry his wife over the story of the wild monkeys in the forest. So, he said absolutely nothing.

In the morning, Mr. Bamboo-Cutter woke up and rubbed his eyes. He wondered if it had all been a dream. So, he decided to go right back to the exact spot where the monkeys had their wild laughing party under the full moon. He rushed there. He looked high and low through all the bamboo, but there was nothing to be seen. This lovely place was very still and quiet, except for a soft wind rustling through the mysterious bamboo.

"So, was it all just a dream?" He felt confused.

Then he said, out loud: "No! No!... I was not dreaming. I definitely saw them!" He made a vow to solve this mystery, and he told himself very seriously, "I will return again and again until I learn the truth about those mischief making monkeys."

The next day he did return, to the exact spot. Nothing. He searched everywhere. No sign at all. But, he was determined, and he returned every single day for the next twenty-seven days. Each day it was the same. No sign of the monkeys. No sign of anything unusual. He only saw the mysterious bamboo.

Then, on the twenty-eighth day, he had a great surprise. It was once again the time of the bright full moon. "Look, there they are!" All of the monkeys were back, and they were just as crazy as ever. They were laughing so hard that they fell to the ground, rolling round and around on the ground.

Mr. Bamboo-Cutter stood very still.

The monkeys were skipping. Monkeys were hopping up and down. Monkeys were pointing and laughing. Squealing with wild excitement they danced in a circle around one glowing, mysterious bamboo in the center of it all. Golden light glowed from this beautiful bamboo. The old Bamboo-Cutter watched the dancing, and he saw all the happy monkey faces smiling in the golden light of the special bamboo. The old man was more than curious now.

"I must get a closer look at that bamboo." said the Bamboo-Cutter.

The wise old man patiently waited, as still as a statue. He was hiding behind some thick trees. Luckily none of the funny monkeys knew he was watching them. He waited behind the trees until every monkey disappeared. Finally, he left his hiding place to get a closer look at this one-of-a-kind bamboo.

"It is something strange and glorious. I am a little afraid." The old man sighed.

Never before in all the long years that the Bamboo-Cutter had lived and worked in the silent bamboo forest had there ever been such a sight. The old man had never felt such curiosity! He approached so slowly and so cautiously. Very carefully, he extended his hand to touch the bamboo of the golden light.

"OUCH!!! Oh, No!" The surface was burning hot!
"Aiiiii, Aiiiii" He cried out in pain.

He tried to pull his hand away, but he could not move.
His hand was stuck to the bamboo.

"Oh, my Goodness! Help! Help!!" he cried. Suddenly he remembered the sharp bamboo knife he always carried. Quickly, he made one perfect, swift cut into the bamboo. Immediately, the top of the bamboo fell to the ground, and then…

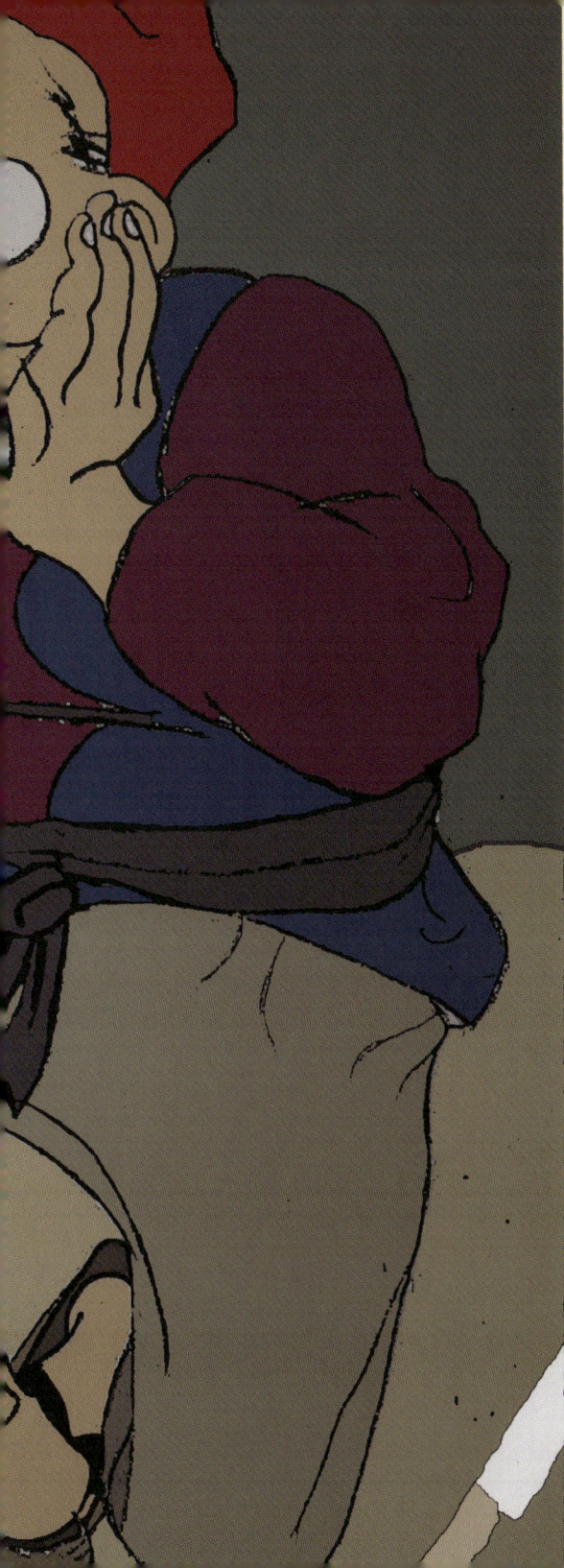

"Oh, my ....my... oh...wow.... Well, my Goodness Gracious..." inside the bamboo he saw that something was moving under the cover of a tiny silk blanket.

"What animal is this? What can it be?" he asked.

He looked more closely, but he could not believe his eyes.
What did he see? He looked more closely, and then he saw a tiny baby.

Bending down, he whispered softly... "Who are you, Little One?"

Gently the old man picked her up with his burnt hand. Immediately, the pain of the burn disappeared. What can this mean? He wondered. What tiny baby has such power? The old man was delighted, but, at the same time, he was so very puzzled.

Smiling, he looked down at the tiny girl in his hand. Then he said, "May I take you home and show you to my wife, Little One?"

The Little One just smiled and laughed.

When Mrs. Bamboo-Cutter saw the baby girl, she was speechless with happiness and surprise. She looked closely at the perfection of this tiny girl.

"Well, My Dear, please tell me, where did you find this perfectly tiny, little girl?"

Her husband, the old Bamboo-Cutter, explained the whole story. He told her about the laughing, crazy monkeys. He told her about the glowing full moon. He told her about the gold bamboo that was so hot to the touch that he could not pull his hand away. The old woman listened to his every word, and then she smiled and laughed.

She said, "I feel certain that the little girl is a gift of Buddha who has heard all our prayers." The old woman's smile was sparkling.

And, so, together they decided to pray again. Her husband also smiled and said, "Well, let us pray together again." The couple sat in front of one of the Bamboo-Cutter's most beautiful Buddha sculptures. It was very fine, and it was made of simple bamboo. With deeply grateful hearts, the old couple prayed: "Oh, Lord Buddha. Our prayers are answered. Thank you for the beautiful baby. We thank you for your kindness to us. We send you millions of thanks for our beautiful, sweet, little girl."

They named her Bamboo Princess.

Bamboo Princess brought so much happiness into the lives of the old man and the old woman. They were no longer lonely. They felt young again because the Princess was always so happy, laughing and playing all day.

Everyday the Princess grew more beautiful. Everyday she grew more kind. She also grew very healthy and strong. By the time she was fourteen years old, the Princess was one of the most charming young ladies in the entire village. Everyone spoke of her kindness and beauty. She seemed to charm every person who met her.

The Princess was devoted to her parents who had been so kind. They were very dear to her heart. Constantly, she tried to think of ways to make them happy. One night on a full moon, she found her parents sitting comfortably outside on a matt. They seemed content as they admired the moonlight together.

"Dear Mama and dear Papa! I would like to entertain you with something special. She spoke with gentle tones, smiling at them.

"Dear Daughter, of course. What is it? We can't wait!"

The surprise was a graceful and elegant dance, more lovely than anything they had ever seen. Something about the dance seemed to create an enchantment. It was a dance of heart-melting beauty. The old couple wondered about this enchanting daughter… she was almost too beautiful….almost too charming.

They watched her dance, just about glued to their seats. They could only stare at her dance in awe and amazement.

"Did you like it?" she asked as she bowed to her parents.

"Like it? Dear One, it is the most beautiful dance we have ever seen. It is unusual and enchanting. It makes us think of shimmering clouds, floating, and circling all around the moon."

"But dear Daughter, please tell us, how did you learn such a dance? This is not a dance from our neighborhood. It is like something out of this world. .. Who taught you to dance like the clouds swirling and floating across the sky?"

For some reason the old couple looked a little worried.

For a moment, Princess Bamboo hesitated.

At last she said, "Dear Parents, I would like to answer your questions, but I cannot. I am sorry. The dance is very secret. I cannot talk about it right now. "She looked at her parents with only a small, sad, smile. "… someday you will know."

Then she gazed lovingly at her aging parents. She knew they were growing older.

"Mother dear, do you feel any pain in your back?" she asked kindly.
Her mother only smiled and said nothing. "Let me tap your shoulder, Mother"

But Mr. Bamboo-Cutter answered for his wife. "She is fine. Please don't worry. I will always take care of her."

"But Father, dear. You look so tired already. You work too hard and your hair is very white." The Princess frowned.

"Sweet Daughter, it is true that we are getting older, but our happiness is growing because of you."

The old couple looked lovingly at one another, and they turned their smiling faces to the Princess. The old man said, "We believe that Buddha brought you to us as an answer to our prayers. Now, let us pray again together: "Numumyo Horengekyo, Numumyo Horengokyo."

As the old man sincerely chanted, he put his hands together, and then he said: "Let us pray that love and peace and healing will spread through our family across the whole world."

At that moment, the old couple noticed the Princess gazing deeply and a little sadly up at the moon.

The Princess suddenly had tears in her eyes because she was thinking about the time when she would have to leave the dear old couple she loved so much.

They did not know what she was thinking, but they worried about the Bamboo Princess as they watched her walk away alone to her room.

Time passed. No more was said of worries or unanswered questions. Life went on as before in the Bamboo-Cutter's house. Everyone worked hard everyday, and everyday the Princess grew in beauty and grace. When she reached the age of twenty-one, everyone in the village was talking about her famous beauty and her kindness to all people. All the young girls wanted to look just like her, and all the young men wanted to marry her.

Young men arrived everyday, carrying loads of sparkling golden treasure and the most extraordinary gifts. The village jeweler brought her a golden sphere covered in precious stones. Another gentleman brought a golden carpet that could fly through the sky and sail over the ocean. A fortune teller brought her a dragon's eye that could see into anyone's former life. A sorcerer brought her a seahorse shaped candle that could fill the sky with rainbows.

But the Princess was not impressed.

The next group to arrive was strong men with astounding physical skills. Each one demonstrated their power in order to win the Princess. A Kung Fu Master was able to demonstrate the power to put wild bears to sleep with his advanced martial arts technique. Another strong man had the power to control enormous, poisonous snakes. Yet another challenger was able to control large bats by forcing them to become stuck to a long stick.

Each man boasted loudly of his strength. Each man proudly claimed that only he could survive any danger.

But again, the Princess was not impressed.

The Princess did not care for expensive glitter and proud boasting. When the Princess sent all of the suitors away, her parents began to worry that she would never marry. The truth was that the Bamboo Princess cared most of all about one thing: and that was the well being of her parents.

For the next seven years there was no more talk of worries and no more talk of marriage for the Princess. Her devotion was to her parents. She did all she could to make them happy, but still she worried about their health.

They never complained, but now they were aging rapidly. She decided that she must find a way to help them. So, she put up a sign asking for someone, a true healer, to come and help. The sign said, "We need someone who has the musical healing hands."

Many hopeful young men arrived with big promises about their healing powers. The Princess knew that a true healer's hands would have a power just like music. She knew that such hands would be so strong and yet so gentle at the same time. Such hands would be soft and also firm. There was one more special fact the Princess understood: the true healer's hands would make wondrous and cheerful sounds when they worked on a person's aches and pains.

Many arrived, but none had the true ability to help her parents. The Princess had very high standards.

Time slipped away until it was only one more day until the Princess' twenty-eighth birthday. On that very day, a humble young man arrived. This healer had gentle eyes and a calm, quiet wisdom.

But! It was not quiet when he worked with his musical hands. He could tap with a sound of low drumming that shook the earth. His healing hands could soothe aches and pains while making the amazing sounds of horses trotting, or stones rolling, or even the sweet sounds of bamboo wind chimes. His strong, healing hands might also make the sounds of thunder and lightening. His hands made a type of art. His fingers could form the shape of a flying butterfly and also the swishing tail of a swimming fish. Next, he might shape his hands to look like moving waves on the ocean.

The Princess was overjoyed.

The kind and talented healer went right to work on the aches and pains of Mr. and Mrs. Bamboo-Cutter. He worked with his musical hands on their shoulders and upper back. The old man felt so much relief. As the healer tapped, the old Bamboo-Cutter listened to the musical sound and felt better than ever.

The old man said, "This is wonderful. I feel so cheerful now. I feel young again."

The old woman's back was bent over with pain until the young healer started his magical work, tapping musically on the aches and pains she felt. She beamed with happiness when she told him that the pain was gone.

"Thank you. Oh, my Goodness, it is delicious to be without pain. Thank you." The old woman giggled like a young girl.

The Princess took the young healer's hands in her own and gazed sweetly into his eyes. "Sir," she said, "may I call you 'Mr. Music Hands Man?'"

He agreed. "Whatever you want is fine with me."

"Anything at all?" the Princess asked.

"Oh, yes. Anything you need." The healer was so kind.

"Please, then, Mr. Music Hands Man, will you stay and live here in our home and care for my parents?"

"Oh, my lovely Princess, I would like that more than anything else!"

The Princess paused a moment and then she said mysteriously, "Yes, but will you stay even though I must leave this place forever?"

"What? I beg your pardon, would you repeat what you just said?" he asked with tones of sadness and confusion in his voice.

The Princess smiled slightly, but she said nothing.

The young healer burst out, "But, what do you mean? What do you mean by that, dear Princess?"

The Princess stayed very quiet, but she told herself how fortunate she was that she found The Music Hands Man to care for her parents.

After all those happy years, now was the sad moment when she had to tell her parents about the secret. Her eyes filled with tears.

"Oh, my dear parents and dear Mr. Music Hands Man, I love you all from the bottom of my heart. I thank you for your great goodness to me. Here is my secret… I could not tell you before, but now you must know. I am from another world, and I was sent here to have the experience of what love is like in a family on earth. I must return very soon to my own home, on the moon. I am a Moon-Maiden. When the moon rises again, my people will come to take me back to the moon where I belong.

Her aged parents were stunned with shock when they heard this story from their Bamboo Princess. They felt grief and confusion. They did not want this moon story to be true. They were confused. They could not hide their growing grief.

The Music Hands Man was ready to take action right away. He asked all the rich and strong men who wanted to marry the Princess to help stop the moon people from taking the Princess away from them.

"Please," he begged, "help me stop them from taking her. Tomorrow the messengers from the moon will come for her. We must stop them. Will you help?"

They all answered loudly, "We will gather a large army to protect the Princess!"

The next evening, a strong army gathered all around to protect the Princess. Some were skeptical about 'the moon people,' but all were ready to fight against any force that might come near the Princess and her family's home. Soldiers were everywhere, surrounding the little house.

Some were up in the trees and others covered the entire rooftop, ready to fight a hundred horses and many soldiers with all their fierce weapons. Inside and around the house other soldiers patrolled every inch of the area.

In the center of the old house, Mr. and Mrs. Bamboo-Cutter and The Music Hands Man sat in a circle around the Princess, praying to Buddha for her protection.

Suddenly the full moon approached, glowing its powerful light all around them all, touching everything with its powerful beams. The moon's light grew stronger and then, suddenly, a great wind blew with terrible force and a blast of rain smashed into the tiny, old house.

The strong men on the roof tried to protect themselves from these fierce winds and rain. Just then, a very bright shooting star hit the top of the roof. Everyone became frozen in one position, except the Princess. In a flash, the winds and the rain stopped. All became very, very quiet. In a moment, the soldiers were free to move again. But, in that very same moment, the Princess had already been carried away. They all looked up, and they could see her floating upwards on a white carpet of clouds. She was already gone. The soldiers were totally powerless.

High above the clouds, the Princess called out to them: "Good-bye, my dear parents, good-bye Mr. Music Hands Man. Thank you. Please take care of my parents. Whenever the moon is full, I will be looking over you. I will be listening to your music hands as you care for my parents until I can return. I love you all. Good-bye! Good-bye!"

The powerful moon forces lifted her higher and higher up into the sky. All they could do was just stand there, watching her float upwards, among the soft clouds, moving towards the lovely full moon.

The people of the village were also very sad that the lovely Princess had left their village and returned to the moon. The story of her kindness was known far and wide. Everyone remembered that she said she would always watch and listen to The Music Hands Man whenever the moon was full. All the children in the village knew the story of the beautiful Princess. They also knew all about the healing powers of The Music Hands Man.

Soon the children followed The Music Hands Man, and he began teaching the children how to practice healing music hands. Soon they could help their own parents and grandparents. Everyday, the children gathered and watched the healer as he worked. He showed them just how to use healing, music hands.

He sang a song for the children to help them remember: "Monday is the day to tap their shoulders, tap their shoulders. This is the way to help your Papa. Tuesday is the day to tap their neck, tap their neck. This is the way to help your Mama every Tuesday." And so on for every day of the week. He taught the children how to tap the shoulders, the upper back, the middle, the lower back and the feet.

Whenever the moon was full, the children gathered under the moonlight so that Princess Bamboo could see how happy and healthy their families were. Since that time, very pretty tapping music comes from every house in the village.

Every boy and every girl practiced the healing music hands on their parents and grandparents to show their appreciation to their elders. No matter what happened to them, the children sincerely expressed their love and gratitude by always helping their elders with the magical, music hands technique.

And, so – this is the wonderful story of the Princess and The Music Hands Man. The story spread across the nation until the Emperor heard the news. He loved the idea of the children helping their families, and he decided to make this a tradition for the whole nation. The Emperor was so glad that elders would have the opportunity to find healing for their aging bodies from the kindness of children using the wisdom they learned from The Music Hands Man. The children gave their help freely unlike the professional therapists who were too expensive for most of the elders. This was the gift of Princess Bamboo and The Music Hands Man.

家族療治
満月時に
曲手施行の事

Since that time, peace and happiness have prevailed in the Emperor's land. The people were calm and friendly. Kids were singing Katatataki music and parents were chanting Num Myoho Renge Kyo. No one even wanted to kill animals. Wars became a thing of the past in this happy, healthy land.

And, do you know? We can all benefit from music hands. Kind children can help their parents to enjoy the experience of peace and healing. This is the best gift of all.

By the way, do you remember those crazy monkeys in the story? Well, every full moon, these monkeys still go wild, jumping up and down all around the bamboo, waiting for the Princess to return.

And indeed, Bamboo Princess did come back to the earth. She returned as a Bodhisattva, practicing Buddhism since then till today as a way to bring happiness to all of us on earth who suffer because of challenging living conditions, sickness, aging and dying. And do you know something? You will also find her within you as you learn to practice her wisdom and her compassion.

The End

Author: DoAnn T. Kaneko

Editor: Dona Snow

Illustrator: Lance Williams

Printed in the United States
135661LV00001B